Holly
the Christmas
Fairy

For Holly Sarah Williams,
my beautiful niece
—D. M.

ISBN 0-439-72402-3

Text copyright © 2004 by Working Partners Limited.

Illustrations copyright © 2004 by Georgie Ripper.

24 23 22 21 20 19 18 17 16 15 14 13   7 8 9/0

Printed in the U.S.A.

First Scholastic printing, December 2004

Holly
the Christmas
Fairy

by Daisy Meadows

Illustrated by Georgie Ripper

SCHOLASTIC INC.

New York Toronto London Auckland Sydney
Mexico City New Delhi Hong Kong Buenos Aires

The Fairyland Palace

Hillfields Farm

Christmas Trees

HILLFIELDS FARM

Tippington Town

Jack Frost's Spell

Christmas plans may go awry,
If I can make these reindeer fly.
Santa's gifts for girls and boys
Shall all become my treats and toys!

Magic reindeer listen well,
As now I bind you with this spell.
Heed my bidding, fly this sleigh
Through starry skies and far away.

Jack Frost is about to ruin Christmas.
Can Rachel and Kirsty stop him with
the help of
Holly the Christmas Fairy?

Contents

A Magical Mistake

"Only three days to go!" Rachel
Walker sighed happily. She was pinning
Christmas cards onto long pieces of red
ribbon, that she was getting ready to
hang on the living room wall. "I *love*
Christmas! Don't you, Kirsty?"

Kirsty Tate, Rachel's best friend,
nodded. "Of course I do," she replied,

handing Rachel another pile of cards.
"It's a *magical* time, isn't it?"

Rachel and Kirsty laughed, and
touched the golden lockets they both
wore around their necks.
The two girls shared a
marvelous, magical
secret. No one else
knew that they were
friends with the fairies!
Kirsty and Rachel had
visited Fairyland several times
when their help had been needed.
The first time, they had rescued the
Rainbow Fairies after they were
banished by Jack Frost's nasty spell. But
then Jack Frost and his goblin servants
had stolen the magic tail feathers from
Doodle, the rooster in charge of fairy

weather. The girls had helped the
Weather Fairies to get Doodle's feathers
back.

In return, the Fairy King and Queen
had given gold lockets to Rachel and
Kirsty. The lockets were full of magic
fairy dust that the girls could use to take
them to Fairyland if ever they needed
help from the fairies.

"Thanks for asking me
to stay," said Kirsty,
cutting another piece
of ribbon. "Mom says
she and Dad will get
me on Christmas Eve."

"We might get some snow before
then!" Rachel smiled. "The weather's
getting much colder. I wonder what
Christmas is like in Fairyland. . . ."

At that moment, the door opened and
Mrs. Walker came in. She was followed by
Buttons, Rachel's friendly, shaggy dog.
He was white with gray patches and had
a long, furry tail.

"Oh, girls, that looks lovely!" Rachel's
mom exclaimed when she saw the cards
hanging on the walls. "We'll go over to
Lakeland Farm and choose a Christmas
tree this evening."

"Hooray!" said Rachel. "Can Kirsty and I decorate it?"

"We were hoping you would!" Her mother laughed. "You'd better get the decorations out of the garage after lunch."

"Buttons seems to love Christmas, too," Kirsty said, smiling. The dog was sniffing around the cards and ribbons.

"He does," Rachel replied. "Every year I buy him some doggie treats and wrap them up. And every year he finds them and eats them before Christmas!"

Buttons wagged his tail. Then he grabbed the end of a ribbon in his mouth and ran off, trailing red ribbon behind him.

"Buttons, no!" Rachel yelled, and she and Kirsty ran after him to get the ribbon back. When the girls had finished hanging the Christmas cards, it was time for a delicious lunch of hot soup. Then Rachel took Kirsty out to the garage to get the decorations.

"It's getting colder," Kirsty said, shivering. "Maybe it *will* snow."

"I hope so," Rachel replied. She switched the garage light on. "The decorations are up there." She pointed at a shelf above the workbench. "I'll stand on the stepladder and hand the boxes down to you."

"OK," Kirsty agreed.

Rachel climbed up the ladder, and began to hand the boxes down. They were full of silver stars, shiny tinsel, and glittering ornaments in pink, purple, and silver.

"I hope you've got a fairy for the top of the tree!" Kirsty joked, as Rachel handed her a box.

"No, we don't!" Rachel laughed. "We've always had a silver star, but it's getting really old and tattered now. Be careful, Kirsty," she warned, lifting another box from the shelf. "This one's got all sorts of things sticking out of it. Oh!" Rachel gasped with surprise. The gold locket around her neck had caught on a little, sparkling wreath made of twigs. The locket burst open, scattering fairy dust all over both girls.

"Oh, no!" Rachel cried, scrambling down from the ladder.

"What should we do?" Kirsty began.

But they didn't have time to do anything. Both girls were suddenly caught up in a swirling cloud of fairy dust that swept them off their feet. The sparkles whirled around them, glittering in the pale winter light.

"Kirsty, we're shrinking!" Rachel cried. "I think we're on our way to Fairyland!"

Christmas Chaos

The girls weren't scared because this had happened to them before. But, as they whirled through the clouds toward Fairyland, Rachel felt a bit embarrassed. She hadn't meant to use her magic fairy dust at all — it was an accident!

"Don't worry," called Kirsty, seeing the

look on Rachel's face. "It'll be
great to see our fairy friends again."

Soon the girls spotted
the red-and-white
toadstool houses of
Fairyland below
them, and then
the silver palace
with its four
pink turrets. As
the girls drifted
closer to the
palace, they could
see a crowd of
fairies waving at
them. There was King
Oberon and Queen Tita-
nia, with the Rainbow
Fairies and all the Weather Fairies, too.

Even Doodle, the fairy rooster, had come to greet them. "Hello!" called Ruby and Saffron. "It's wonderful to see you!" cried Pearl and Storm. As the girls landed on the ground, the fairies crowded around them. Rachel quickly tried to explain. "I'm sorry," she said. "We didn't mean to come. It was an accident."

The queen smiled. "No, it *wasn't* an accident!" she said in her silvery voice. "Our magic made your locket open. I'm afraid we need your help again, girls!"

The two friends turned to stare at each other in surprise, their eyes wide.

"Not Jack Frost again?" Kirsty asked.

"Hasn't he been banished to the end of the rainbow?" Rachel added.

"We'll tell you all about it," replied
the queen. "But first . . ."
She waved her wand
at Rachel's locket. It
filled with fairy dust
again, and closed,
all on its own.

"Now," the king
said, turning to the fairies.
"Where is Holly the Christmas Fairy?"

Kirsty and Rachel watched eagerly as
Holly came forward. They had never met
the Christmas Fairy before. She had long
dark hair, and she wore a little red dress,
exactly the same color as a holly berry.
The dress had a hood with furry white
trim, and she wore tiny red boots. But
although she was the Christmas Fairy,
Holly looked rather sad.

"Holly is in charge of putting the sparkle into Christmas," Queen Titania explained.

"That's right." Holly sighed. "I organize Santa's elves, and I teach the reindeer to fly. It's my job to make sure that Christmas is as sparkly and happy as possible."

"But this year Jack Frost is causing trouble," the king told them. "We let him come back from the end of the rainbow because he said he was sorry and he promised to behave."

"And we agreed that he could help Doodle with the wintry weather," said Queen Titania.

"So what happened?" Rachel asked.

"Well, Jack Frost sent a letter to Santa Claus asking for presents," the king went on. "But he got a letter back saying he'd been so naughty, he wouldn't be getting anything this year!"

"We'll show you what Jack Frost did next," said the queen. She waved her wand over a small pool of blue water that lay among the flowers. The water bubbled and fizzed, and then became smooth as glass.

Pictures began to appear on the surface. Kirsty and Rachel saw a large log cabin at nighttime. It was surrounded by deep snow, and icicles hung from the wooden roof. Inside, the cabin was full of toys. There were dolls, bikes, games, puzzles,

and books, all lying around in huge piles.
Kirsty and Rachel had never seen so
many toys.

"Oh!" Kirsty gasped, her hand flying to
her mouth. "Rachel, look!"

In the corner of the cabin stood a
beautiful wooden rocking horse.
Someone was painting gold patterns onto
the rockers. He was all dressed in red and
white, and he had a jolly face with a
long white beard.

"It's Santa!" Rachel cried happily.

Then the picture changed to show the outside of the cabin again. There the girls could see Santa's sleigh. It was silver and white, and sparkled with magic. Eight reindeer were harnessed to the sleigh, all ready to go. They were waiting patiently, shaking their antlers every so often.

Lots of little elves wearing bright green tunics scurried around the sleigh, filling it with presents. The bells on the tips of their hats tinkled merrily as they rushed here and there with armfuls of packages.

Kirsty and Rachel were so delighted, they almost forgot why they were watching. But then, just as the sleigh was full to bursting with presents, the thin, spiky figure of Jack Frost appeared.

As Kirsty and Rachel watched, Jack Frost peeped out from behind the log cabin. When there were no elves near the sleigh, he ran over to it and jumped in. Grabbing the reins, he shouted a spell to make the reindeer obey him. And the next moment, the sleigh lifted off the ground and zoomed away into the starry night sky.

As soon as the elves saw what was
happening, they chased
after him, but the
magic sleigh was
much too fast for
them to catch.

"Oh, how could he?" Kirsty said
angrily. "He's stolen Santa's sleigh!"

"So now you see why we need your
help," said Queen Titania, as the pictures
faded away. "Holly must find Santa's
sleigh and return it before Christmas Eve,
or Christmas will be ruined for all the
children around the world!"

"We think Jack Frost has taken the
sleigh to *your* world," Holly added. "He
loves parties, so he won't want to miss
Christmas. Will you help me?"

"Of course we will," Rachel and Kirsty replied together.

Holly smiled. "Thank you!" she cried, giving both girls a hug.

"Where should we start looking?" asked Rachel.

"As always, the magic will come to you," Titania said with a smile. "You'll know when you are on the right track. And Holly will help. But there is one more thing you need to know. . . ." The queen waved her wand over the pool once more, and the girls watched as an

image of three presents appeared. They
were wrapped in beautiful golden paper,
and tied with big bows that glittered in
all the colors of the rainbow.

"These three presents are very special,"
the queen explained. "So please try to
find them."

"We'll do our best," said Kirsty, and
Rachel nodded.

The king stepped forward, holding a
soft golden bag. "This can help you to
defeat Jack Frost," he said, opening the
bag and showing the girls a sparkling
fairy crown. "It has powerful magic. If

Jack Frost puts it on, he will immediately be brought here to appear before the queen and me."

Kirsty took the bag and put the strap safely over her shoulder.

"Good luck, Rachel and Kirsty!" called the queen. She raised her wand and sent another shower of fairy dust whirling and swirling around the girls. Rachel and Kirsty were lifted off their feet to begin the journey home.

Buttons on the Loose!

"We're back!" Rachel said, as the sparkling clouds of fairy dust cleared. They were in the Walkers' garage again.

"And we're back to normal size," Kirsty added, brushing a speck of fairy dust from her jeans. "Poor Holly. I hope we can help."

"We'll find that horrible Jack Frost!" said Rachel. "But we'd better take these decorations inside now. Mom will be wondering where we've been."

Kirsty popped the tiny golden bag into her pocket for safekeeping. Then she helped Rachel carry the boxes into the house. There they started looking through the decorations.

"I see what you mean
about the star," Kirsty
said, holding up a
large but tattered
silver star.
"Maybe Mom will
let me buy something
new for the top of the
tree," replied Rachel. "I'd love to have a
fairy this year!"

The girls spent the afternoon sorting
out the decorations. Rachel's dad arrived
home from work at six o'clock, and then
they all went to Hillfields Farm to choose
the Christmas tree.

"It looks like everyone had the same
idea!" remarked Rachel's mom, as the car
drew up outside the farm. Lots of people
were looking at Christmas trees. There

seemed to be hundreds of trees in all
shapes and sizes.

"At least there are plenty of them!"
Kirsty laughed.

"And we'll find the *perfect* one," said
Rachel, climbing out of the car.

The two girls hurried over to the
farmyard, while Mr. and Mrs. Walker
followed with Buttons. The evening was
cold and clear, and stars glittered in the
dark sky.

"Don't choose one that's too big," called Mrs. Walker. "We'll never get it through the front door."

Rachel and Kirsty wandered up and down the rows of trees. But they couldn't seem to find one that was just right. They were either too big, too small, too bushy, or too thin.

Then one tree caught Rachel's eye just ahead of her. The needles were so green and shiny, they almost seemed to glow in the frosty air. *"That tree looks perfect,"* she said to herself, as she went over to it. *"It's not too big and it's not too small."* Suddenly, Rachel

spotted a bright red glow, right in the
middle of the tree. Then a tiny face
peeped out at her.

"It's me!" Holly cried, waving her wand
and sending little sparkly red holly berries
bouncing around the tree.

Rachel laughed. "Kirsty, over here!" she
called.

Kirsty rushed over. "What are you
doing here, Holly?" she asked. "Is Jack
Frost close by?"

But before Holly could answer, there was a shout from Mrs. Walker, and Buttons dashed past the girls, his leash trailing along behind him. He was barking loudly.

"Stop him, girls!" puffed Mrs. Walker. "I don't know what's the matter with him. He pulled the leash right out of my hand."

"We'll catch him, Mom," Rachel called. "You look after our tree."

Holly hopped inside Kirsty's pocket, and then the girls ran after the excited dog. Buttons had left the farmyard, and was racing toward an oak tree.

Suddenly, Kirsty saw a shadow dodge out
from behind the tree, and head
for an old barn. Although
it was dark, she could
just about make out a
sharp, pointed nose
and big feet.

 "Oh!" She gasped.
"I think Buttons is
chasing one of Jack
Frost's goblins!"

 "I knew they were
around here somewhere!"
Holly cried. "Quick! After him!"

 Buttons was standing outside
the barn, sniffing at the door.

 "The goblin must be inside," Rachel
whispered, grabbing the dog's leash.
Quickly, she hooked it over a nail

sticking out of the barn wall,
and gave him a pat.
"Wait here quietly,
Buttons," she whispered.
"We won't be long."

"Let's look inside," Kirsty
said. She edged the barn door
open and they all peeked in.

A cold blast of icy air swirled around
them. The girls and Holly could see
across the barn to the large doors at the
opposite end. Those doors were wide
open, and a sparkling trail led out of the
barn and right up into the sky. At the far
end of the trail, they could make out a
glittering silver shape traveling very fast.
It was Santa's missing sleigh!

Grumpy Goblins

"Jack Frost *was* here," Kirsty said, looking disappointed. "We just missed him."

"That's why it's so cold," Holly agreed with a shiver.

The barn was full of bales of hay, and looking around, Rachel noticed that there was wrapping paper scattered all over them. "Jack Frost has been opening Santa's presents!" she said angrily. "Isn't he mean?"

"Ssh!" Holly whispered. "Goblins!"

Two goblins had just rolled out from behind one of the hay bales near the

open doors. They were fighting and yelling at each other.

"It's mine!" shouted one with a wart on his nose.

"No, it's mine!" yelled the other.

"Look," Rachel said. She pointed at the present the goblins were arguing over. "It's

one of the three special presents the
queen asked us to look for!"

"We have to get that back," said Holly.

"The other two presents must still be on
the sleigh," Kirsty
added. "I don't see that
special gold wrap-
ping paper
anywhere."

The goblins were
still fighting,
rolling around on
the dusty floor of
the barn.

"Give it to me!"
yelled the warty
one. "There might be
Christmas cake inside, or gin-
ger snaps, or yummy apple pies, or —"

"Apple pies!" the other goblin cried, licking his lips. "I'm going to eat them all!"

"What are we going to do?" Rachel whispered. "How are we going to get the present back?" Kirsty frowned. "I've got an idea," she said. "Holly, could you use your magic to create the smell of hot apple pie?" Holly's eyes twinkled. "Of course," she replied.

"We'll tell the goblins there's a big plate of apple pie in the hayloft," Kirsty went on. "They're so greedy, they're bound to go and look. And they can't climb the

ladder *and* hang on to the present. We'll
be able to grab it!"

Rachel and Holly beamed at her.

"Great idea!" said Holly. "One magic
smell of hot apple pie coming up!" And
she flew toward the goblins.

Holly's Magic Trick

Rachel and Kirsty watched anxiously as Holly fluttered over the goblins' heads. They were so busy fighting, they didn't notice her.

Holly waved her wand in the air, and a few seconds later the smell of freshly baked apple pie began to waft around the barn. Even Rachel and Kirsty, who were standing outside, could smell it.

The goblins stopped fighting. They lifted their big noses into the air and sniffed hard.

"Fresh apple pie!" Holly called, and she pointed at the ladder to the hayloft. "Up in the hayloft. Help yourselves."

"Apple pie! Yum!" shouted the warty goblin. He shoved the present at the other goblin, and dashed for the ladder. But the other one didn't want to be left behind. He raced over to the ladder, too, hot on the heels of the warty goblin. As soon as he realized that he couldn't climb up to the hayloft with the present in his arms, he threw it down on a pile of straw.

Rachel and Kirsty laughed to themselves, as they watched the goblins scrambling up the ladder and trying to shove each other out of the way. When they had reached the top, the girls dashed into the barn and Kirsty picked up the present.

45

Suddenly there was a shout from above. "There aren't any apple pies here!"

"We've been tricked!"

One of the goblins peered down into the barn. "Where's that tricky little fairy?" he yelled.

"Quick!" Holly gasped. "Let's get out of here!"

The girls and Holly dashed for the door as the goblins tumbled down the ladder.

"After them!" the warty goblin shouted.

Outside the barn Rachel fumbled to
free Buttons's leash from
the nail. The goblins
appeared in the
doorway and ran
toward her. But
Buttons began to bark
loudly as soon as he saw
them. The goblins looked wary.

"*You* get the present back!" the warty
one yelled, nudging the other.

"No, *you* get it!" the other goblin shouted.

Still barking, Buttons began pulling
Rachel toward them. Immediately, the
two terrified goblins shot back into the
barn and shut the door.

"Good dog!" said Rachel, patting
Buttons to calm him down. Meanwhile,
Kirsty handed the present to Holly.

"Hurray! We've found one special present," Holly beamed, clutching the package. "I'll take this back to Fairyland right away."

"We'll see you again soon," Rachel called, as Holly fluttered up into the sky.

"I'll be back as soon as I find out where Jack Frost is!" Holly promised.

Rachel and Kirsty hurried back to the farmyard to find Mr. and Mrs. Walker. They had bought the tree Rachel had chosen, and were tying it to the roof of the car.

"Now, I think it's time we all went home and had some apple pie and hot chocolate," said Rachel's mom, as they climbed into the car.

Rachel and Kirsty grinned at each other.

"Apple pie would be perfect, Mom," said Rachel, trying not to laugh.

"I think Buttons deserves a piece of apple pie, too," Kirsty whispered. "After all, he was the one who led us to the goblins and the first present."

"Woof!" Buttons agreed.

"Yes, and our fairy adventures aren't over yet," Rachel said, her eyes shining. "This is going to be the most exciting Christmas *ever*!"

Christmas Shopping

"Two days till Christmas!" Rachel said the next morning, as she stood in front of the bedroom mirror, brushing her hair. The girls were getting ready to go Christmas shopping with Rachel's mom. "Isn't it exciting, Kirsty?"

Kirsty nodded. "I can't wait!" she said. "But I don't want it to arrive too soon.

We have to find Jack Frost and Santa's sleigh first."

"I know," Rachel agreed. "Once we've helped our fairy friends, then we can *really* start to enjoy Christmas."

"I need to buy a present for my mom," Kirsty went on. "Do you have many presents left to buy?"

Rachel shook her head. "Only one," she

 replied. "But the mall has fantastic Christmas displays, so it's fun to look around, even if you haven't got much shopping to do."

"Girls, are you ready yet?" Mrs. Walker called up the stairs.

"Coming, Mom," Rachel yelled back.

The girls clattered downstairs, laughing and chatting. Mrs. Walker was waiting for them in the hall. "Don't forget your scarves and gloves," she said, picking up her car keys. "It's absolutely freezing today, and the mall parking lot is outside." She opened the front door, and went to get the car from the garage.

Rachel shivered as a blast of cold air swept through the open door, and rustled through the tinsel on the Christmas

tree. "Brr!" she gasped, grabbing her coat.
"Mom's right. It *is* cold today."

"Doesn't the tree look fantastic?" asked
Kirsty admiringly, pulling on her gloves.
The Walkers had a large entrance hall and
they had put the tree in a corner near the
stairs. Rachel and Kirsty had decorated it

beautifully, and now it glittered and gleamed with ornaments, tinsel, and lights.

"It's the nicest one we've ever had," Rachel agreed. "But I'll switch the lights off now that we're going out."

Kirsty watched as Rachel switched off the Christmas tree lights, and then she

noticed that something was different about the tree. Instead of the tired and tattered silver star, which she had carefully placed on the top, there now sat a beautiful, sparkly fairy! As Kirsty stared in surprise, she realized that it was a *real* fairy. Holly was perched at the top of the tree, glowing brightly in her berry-red dress, and waving at Kirsty. "Holly!" Kirsty laughed. "What are you doing up there?"

"I thought your tree was missing a fairy!" Holly grinned.

Rachel looked up to see Holly fly down from the tree and land on Kirsty's shoulder. "Hello, Rachel," sang Holly in her pretty, tinkly voice. "I have a feeling something magical is going to happen today, so can I come to the shops with you?"

"Of course," Rachel replied happily. "But you'll have to hide from my mom!"

"No problem." Holly winked at the
girls, and snuggled down inside Kirsty's
coat pocket, folding her wings away
neatly. She popped out a second later to
say, "Don't forget the magic crown!"

"It's in my pocket," Rachel assured her.

Then they heard Rachel's mom toot
the car horn.

"Maybe something magical *is* going to happen!" Rachel whispered to Kirsty, as they rushed outside. "Maybe we'll get Santa's sleigh *and* the two special presents back today."

"I hope so!" Kirsty agreed with a smile.

A Chilling Suspicion

Although it was still early in the morning, the mall was already busy when they arrived. Mrs. Walker had to wait in a line to get into the parking lot, and it took them quite a while to find an empty space.

"Now then, Rachel," she said, as they all climbed out of the car, "would you and Kirsty like to go shopping on your own? I have some presents to buy that I don't want you to see!"

"Like what?" Rachel asked curiously.

Her mom laughed. "If I tell you, they won't be a surprise, will they?" she said. "We'll split up, and I'll meet you and Kirsty in an hour by the glass elevators. Make sure you stay inside the mall."

"OK," the girls agreed.

Mrs. Walker went to get the elevator, while the girls stayed on the ground floor. They walked through the mall, looking at the Christmas displays in the shop windows and chatting happily.

Christmas songs were playing over the speaker system, and people were bustling to and fro carrying lots of shopping bags.

Rachel and Kirsty had soon bought the few presents they had left to get. Kirsty bought some pretty silver earrings for her mom, and Rachel bought a diary for her dad.

"Are you OK in there, Holly?" Kirsty whispered, putting the earrings into her other pocket.

Holly nodded. She was peeping out from Kirsty's pocket to see what was going on. But she was so small, nobody noticed her among the hustle and bustle.

"Come and see the mall's main Christmas display," Rachel said to Kirsty. "It's beautiful."

Kirsty nodded eagerly, and Rachel led the way to the big central square of the shopping mall. There, right in front of them, was Santa's Village.

"Wow!" said Kirsty, her eyes wide. "This is fantastic!"

The village had a huge white tent
covered in sparkling lights that changed
color from white to blue to silver and
then back again. Long, glittering
icicles hung from the roof. The
tent was surrounded by
fake snow, and
there were life-size
toy polar bears
and penguins that
waved at the
shoppers going
by. Near the
tent was a
small ice rink. Boys
and girls dressed as elves
were skating all around it, some carrying
brightly wrapped presents, others
performing acrobatics and tumbles. A

pretty little bridge made of sparkling icicles led the way into the village.

"Isn't it beautiful?" Rachel said, as they moved closer to get a better look.

There was a long line of children waiting to see Santa. Rachel and Kirsty were standing near the bridge, watching the elves on the ice skating rink, when a little girl ran out of the tent to join her mom. She seemed upset and Kirsty and Rachel couldn't help overhearing what she said.

"Did you have a good time, darling?" the mother asked.

"Well, Santa's sleigh was all bright and sparkly," the little girl told her breathlessly, "and his reindeer were furry and friendly. But Santa wasn't very nice!" She stuck her bottom lip out as if she was about to cry. "He wouldn't let me have a present, even though he had lots and lots. And he was all cold and spiky!"

Immediately, Rachel's ears pricked up. That didn't sound like Santa at all. But it did sound like someone else she knew — someone mean and tricky and cunning. Rachel thought they might have just found Jack Frost!

Not the Real Santa!

"Kirsty!" Rachel said, pulling her friend to one side so their conversation wouldn't be overheard. "Did you and Holly hear that? I think Jack Frost might be inside the tent, pretending to be Santa!"

Kirsty stared at Rachel. "You could be right!" she gasped.

"Yes," Holly piped up. "We'd better check it out."

"How are we going to get into the tent?" asked Rachel. "It'll take ages if we stand in line."

"She's right," Kirsty said. "Let's try to slip around the back and see what's going on."

The girls crept around the back of the tent, keeping a sharp eye out for anyone who might try to stop them. But they found the tent was tied down so firmly, they couldn't sneak underneath.

"Leave this to me!" Holly whispered. She waved her wand, and a shower of sparkling red fairy dust fell onto a corner of the tent. Immediately, the ropes loosened, and that part of the canvas curled upward.

"Thanks, Holly!" said Rachel. "Come on, Kirsty."

The two girls crept cautiously under the edge of the tent. Inside were lots of glittering ice-covered rocks. Rachel, Kirsty, and Holly hid behind them while they looked around.

The tent was lit with magical, rainbow-colored lanterns that glowed in the dim interior. Long, gleaming icicles hung from the ceiling, and a big Christmas tree stood in one corner, decorated with shiny silver crystals and multicolored fairy lights.

Kirsty shivered. The air inside the tent felt cold and frosty. "It's really chilly in here," she whispered. "Jack Frost must be nearby."

And, sure enough, there, in the middle
of the room, was Santa's beautiful
sparkling sleigh, complete with hundreds
of presents, eight magic reindeer, and Jack
Frost! He was ripping open a present,
although the ground in front of him was
already littered with discarded wrapping
paper. He wore a red Santa suit and a big
fake white beard. But he still looked like
his mean, cold, spiky self. "Bring me

another!" he roared, tossing aside the game of *Chutes and Ladders* he'd just opened.

His goblin servants came rushing from every corner of the village. They were all carrying presents, which they pushed into Jack Frost's greedy hands. Rachel and Kirsty held their breath nervously as goblins hurried past their hiding place.

Suddenly Kirsty spotted something. "Look!" she hissed, pointing at the sleigh. "It's one of the special presents!" The gold-wrapped package was sitting at the back of the sleigh, on top of a pile of other toys.

"You're right," Holly whispered excitedly. "And the third one must still be on the sleigh somewhere, too. It doesn't look as though Jack Frost has already opened it."

"But how are we going to get hold of them without Jack Frost and his goblins spotting us?" Rachel asked anxiously.

"If we stay behind the rocks, we can crawl around to the back of the sleigh without being seen," said Kirsty.

"And I can help you," Holly added eagerly. "I'll distract Jack Frost and the goblins."

"What are you going to do?" asked Kirsty.

"I'll use my magic to put myself inside one of the presents that Jack Frost is opening," Holly replied. "That'll give him a shock!"

"That's a great idea," Rachel declared. "Now, we'll creep up to the back of the sleigh. Then, while Holly creates a diversion, you grab the present, Kirsty, and I'll try to drop the magic crown on Jack Frost's head."

"OK. Let's go," Kirsty whispered.

Holly nodded. She waved her wand above her head and immediately disappeared.

Rachel and Kirsty began to crawl on their hands and knees toward the sleigh, keeping out of sight behind the rocks. Jack Frost was far too busy unwrapping presents to notice them.

And, luckily, the goblins were preoccupied with running backward and forward, trying to keep their grumpy master happy.

Their hearts thumping, the girls drew
nearer to the sleigh. The special present
was so close now that Kirsty could reach
out and touch it.

"Now we just wait for Holly to make
her move," Rachel whispered.

The girls watched Jack

Frost ripping the paper off yet another
gift. "I'm bored," he grumbled coldly.
"Why can't I get a really *nice* present?"
He threw the paper on the floor, and held
up a pretty wooden box. "I wonder
what's in here?" he muttered.

Suddenly, the lid of the
box burst open. Holly
shot out in a huge
shower of glittering
red holly berries
and fairy dust,
making Jack Frost
and the goblins
cough and splutter.

"This is our chance!" Kirsty said to
Rachel, as Jack Frost and his goblins
stared at Holly in stunned surprise.

Rachel nodded and together the girls
moved toward Jack Frost.

The Chase is On

Kirsty stretched out her hand for the special present. Meanwhile, Rachel pulled the crown out of her pocket, and stood up, ready to drop it onto the fake Santa's head.

"What's going on?" Jack Frost shouted, still rubbing fairy dust out of his eyes. "It's that pesky Christmas Fairy, isn't it? Grab her!"

Kirsty had her hands on the present now, and Rachel was leaning over the sleigh with the crown. But just then, one of the goblins spotted her. "Look out!" he screeched, pointing a bony finger at Rachel.

Jack Frost spun around. His cold, hard eyes met Rachel's and she felt herself shiver. Quickly, Jack Frost waved his wand, and immediately the reindeer galloped off, pulling the sleigh behind

them. Luckily, Kirsty was still hanging
onto the ribbon of the present.
As the sleigh moved away,
the present tumbled off
the back and fell safely
into her arms.

"I want you to
grab that fairy!"
Jack Frost
roared at his
goblin
servants as
the reindeer
galloped toward
the tent entrance,
taking the sleigh with
them. "And those interfering
girls, too!"

"Kirsty! Rachel!" shouted Holly,

who was zooming up and away from the
goblins. "You've got to get out of here!"

The reindeer galloped out of the tent
and flew up into the air above the
shoppers. As the sleigh soared overhead,
the shoppers looked up in amazement.
They gasped, and then began clapping
and cheering, thinking it was some sort of
fabulous Christmas magic show.

The sleigh flew through the mall and out of the big double doors. Meanwhile, the goblins were closing in on the girls, backing them into a corner of the tent. "We've got you now!" one of them snarled.

"You can't get the better of *us*!" boasted another.

Kirsty and Rachel felt very scared. "Split up and run for it, when I give the word!" Rachel whispered. She waited until the goblins were quite close, and then shouted, "Now!"

Immediately, she and Kirsty ran as
fast as they could in opposite directions.
The goblins chased after them, but there
was a lot of pushing and shoving and
shouting as the clumsy goblins bumped
into one another and tripped over their
own feet.

In the middle of the chaos, Rachel and Kirsty both headed for the doorway. Kirsty reached it first. She noticed that Rachel was nearly at the exit, too, but a goblin was very close behind her, and as Kirsty slipped out of the tent, she saw the goblin reach for her friend!

The Great Escape

The goblin missed Rachel and fell over,
tripping up another goblin who was hot
on his heels. The girls had escaped from
the tent, but they knew that the goblins
were right behind them. They had hardly
any time to get away.

"Quick, Kirsty!" Rachel shouted.

"Those support ropes at the back of the tent — we need to pull them out!"

Kirsty knew exactly what Rachel had in mind. The two girls began pulling and heaving at the ropes with all their might.

Suddenly, there was a creaking sound and the ropes gave way. The large white tent wobbled a little and then fell to the ground, trapping the goblins underneath the heavy white canvas.

"We did it!" Kirsty gasped. "Great job, Rachel. That was a wonderful idea!"

"Yes, but I think we'd better get out of here before those goblins escape," Rachel whispered. "It's almost time to meet Mom anyway."

"Where's Holly?" asked Kirsty, looking around.

"Here I am!" called a tiny, silvery voice, and Holly zoomed over to land on Kirsty's shoulder. All the shoppers were too busy staring at the collapsed tent to notice the tiny fairy.

"Are you all right?" Rachel asked anxiously.

"I'm fine," Holly beamed. "Thank you for getting the second present. The Fairy King and Queen *will* be pleased!"

Kirsty held the present out and Holly waved her wand over it. Fairy dust fluttered down around it and the present promptly vanished back to Fairyland.

"I *almost* got the crown on Jack Frost's head!" Rachel sighed, as she put it carefully back into her pocket. "But he got away again. And we don't know where he's gone."

"Oh, yes, we do!" Holly told her excitedly. "While you were escaping from the goblins, I followed the sleigh and spoke to one of my reindeer friends."

"What did he say?" asked Rachel eagerly.

"He told me Jack Frost is really annoyed that we keep finding him in the human world," Holly explained. "He wants to open all of Santa's presents in peace and quiet. So he's told the reindeer to take him to his ice castle right away."

"His ice castle!" Kirsty exclaimed. "Is that where Jack Frost lives?"

Holly nodded.

"Do you know where it is, Holly?" Rachel asked.

"Yes," Holly replied. "It's a cold, scary place, but I can take you there tomorrow, if you still want to help?"

"Of course we do!" said Kirsty and Rachel together.

Holly beamed at them. "Then I'll whiz back to Fairyland now and report to the king and queen," she went on. "Can you get me out of this shopping mall?"

"Of course," Kirsty said, smiling. While Holly hid under Kirsty's scarf, the girls walked quickly over to one of the doors that led out into the parking lot. When nobody was looking, Holly slipped out from under the scarf, gave the girls a cheery wave, and then zoomed up into the sky. The girls watched her fly away until she was out of sight.

Then they hurried back through the
mall toward the glass elevators,
where they had promised to
meet Rachel's mom.

Mrs. Walker was already waiting for
them, holding lots of
shopping bags.
"Hello, girls,"
she smiled.
"I thought
you were lost!
Did you get
everything
you wanted?"
"Almost!"
Rachel replied,
with a quick
glance at Kirsty.

"Well, did you see Santa's village?"
Mrs. Walker continued, leading the way
back to the car. "I heard it was very
beautiful — until it collapsed! But some
of the parents were complaining that
Santa Claus was rather grumpy."

Rachel and Kirsty
grinned at each
other. "He was!"
Kirsty agreed.

"I wonder
what's going
to happen
tomorrow,
Rachel," Kirsty
whispered as Mrs.
Walker unlocked the car.
"Jack Frost's ice castle sounds scary."

"I know," Rachel whispered back. "But we can't let our fairy friends down."

"No," Kirsty agreed firmly. "We have to get Santa's sleigh *and* the third present."

"And this time we'll get that magic crown on Jack Frost's head!" added Rachel. The girls exchanged a determined smile and climbed into the car, feeling very excited and a little bit nervous about just what tomorrow might have in store!

Winter Wonderland

Rachel opened her eyes and yawned. She sat up in bed and looked across at Kirsty, who was still asleep. "Tonight is Christmas Eve!" Rachel said to herself excitedly. But it would only be a merry Christmas if they managed to get Santa's sleigh and all the presents back to Santa today. If they didn't, greedy Jack Frost would spoil everything.

Rachel pushed back the blanket and shivered. Even though the heat was on, there was still a chill in the air. She went across to the window and looked outside. "Oh!" She gasped.

It had snowed heavily during the night, and the trees, the lawn, and the bushes were all hidden under a thick blanket of sparkling white snow.

"What is it?" Kirsty yawned.

"Sorry, did I wake you?" asked
Rachel. "I was just so surprised to see
the snow."

"Snow!" Kirsty
gasped. She
jumped out
of bed and
ran over to
join Rachel.
They both
peered out of
the frosty window.

"It looks like we're
going to have a white
Christmas." Rachel smiled.

"It'll be the best Christmas ever," Kirsty
agreed, "as long as we make it back from
Jack Frost's ice castle. . . ."

"Are you scared?" asked Rachel.

"A bit," Kirsty replied. "But I'm not giving up. Are you?"

"No way!" Rachel laughed. "Come on. Let's get dressed and have breakfast. Then we can go outside."

The two girls hurried downstairs for scrambled eggs and toast. Then they put

on their coats and boots, and ran out into the yard. Their feet sank into the soft snow, leaving tracks all over the lawn. It started snowing again, and pretty snowflakes drifted down around them.

Kirsty rolled a snowball in her hands. "Let's have a snowball fight!" She grinned and threw it at Rachel.

Laughing, Rachel ducked, but before the snowball reached her, it exploded in the air like a firework. Tiny sparkling icicles of red fire shot in all directions. As Kirsty and Rachel watched in amazement, Holly burst out of the snowball.

"Here I am!" she cried, shaking snowflakes from her red dress. "Are you ready, girls? It's time to go to Jack Frost's ice castle!"

The Ice Castle

"We're ready!" Rachel said bravely.

Kirsty nodded and checked her pocket to make sure she had the magic crown.

Then Holly waved her wand in the air. Berry-red fairy dust drifted down over the girls, and they began to shrink. In a moment, they were fairy-size with thin, gauzy wings on their backs.

Holly fluttered up into the air, and Rachel and Kirsty followed her.

"Here we go!" Holly said, waving her wand again.

It was snowing quite heavily now, and the falling snowflakes began to spin and dance around the girls until Rachel and Kirsty couldn't see anything at all.

Then, the blizzard of snow cleared as quickly as it had begun. Rachel and Kirsty gasped. They were no longer in the Walkers' back-yard. Instead, they were standing in a tree, star-ing up at Jack Frost's ice castle.

The castle stood on a tall hill, under a gloomy, gray winter sky. It was built from sheets of ice, and it had four towers tipped with icy blue turrets. The ice glittered and gleamed like diamonds, but the palace still looked cold and scary.

"Be careful," Holly whispered, as a couple of goblins wandered underneath the tree. "There are goblins every-where. We'll never get in through the main gate."

"Maybe we can find a way in from the towers," Rachel suggested, looking upward.

"Good idea," Holly replied. "Follow me." The girls followed Holly as she flew up toward one of the ice-blue turrets. "See what I mean?" Holly said quietly. Rachel and Holly peered down at the castle beneath them.

Holly was right. There were goblin guards at every door.

"Maybe we can find an open window," whispered Rachel.

Holly nodded. "Let's split up and take a look.

We'll meet back here in a few minutes."

They flew off in different directions. Kirsty went to look around the tops of the towers, one by one.

There were lots of windows, but all of them were locked. She flew back to meet Rachel and Holly.

Rachel was already waiting. "I didn't have any luck," she sighed. "Did you?"

Kirsty shook her head sadly.

At that moment, Holly fluttered down to join them.

"You took a long time," said Kirsty.

"I had to hide from one of the goblins," Holly explained. "He was marching along the towers on guard duty."

"We didn't find any open windows,"
Rachel told her. "Did you?"

Holly shook her head. "No, but I
found another way in!" She grinned.
"Follow me!"

Holly led the girls to a place on the
turrets and pointed
at the icy floor.
"Look!" she said.

"A trapdoor!"
Kirsty gasped.

Holly nodded.
"When I was
hiding from the
goblin, I saw him
lift the trapdoor and
go into the castle," she
told them. "And I don't
think he bolted it on the other side."

111

They checked that there were no
goblins around, and then flew down to
the trapdoor. It was a slab of ice with a
steel ring in the top.

"It looks very heavy," Rachel said with
a frown.

"That's no problem," Holly said,
smiling. She waved her wand and the
trapdoor suddenly flew open in a whirl of
fairy dust.

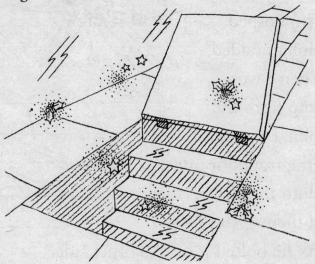

Below were steps of ice, leading down into the castle. Shivering with cold, Rachel, Kirsty, and Holly flew inside.

"We have to start looking for Santa's sleigh right away," Holly whispered to the girls.

"It's not easy to hide a sleigh and eight reindeer!" said Rachel thoughtfully.

"Maybe they're in the stables?" Kirsty suggested.

"That's a good place to start," said Holly. "But keep a sharp lookout for goblins!"

The friends flew down the winding
staircase toward the ground floor of the
castle. But as they fluttered around a
corner of the stairs, they bumped right
into a goblin who was on his way up.

"Fairies!" roared the goblin furiously.
"What are you doing here?" He grabbed
at Holly, but missed as she darted out of
reach. "Help! Fairies!" he shouted.

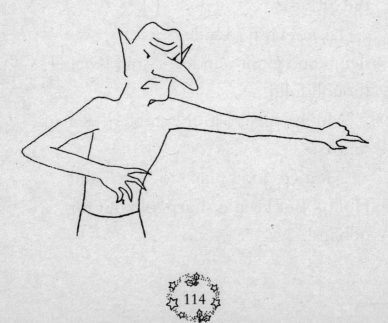

Holly, Rachel, and Kirsty turned and whizzed back up the stairs. But as they reached the next corner, they heard the loud clatter of footsteps. Six more goblins were rushing toward them!

Capture!

The friends tried to dodge out of the
way, but they were completely
surrounded by goblins. Holly and Rachel
were grabbed immediately. Kirsty tried to
fly away overhead, but one goblin
jumped onto another's shoulders and
caught hold of her ankle.

The goblins laughed gleefully. "Now

you're our prisoners!" they said, gloating.
"Jack Frost is going to be very pleased
with us!"

The goblins took the friends through
the ice castle and into the Great Hall. It
was a huge room carved from shining
sheets of ice. At one end was Jack Frost's
throne. It looked very grand, made out of
glittering icicles that had been twisted
into shape.

But Jack Frost wasn't sitting on his throne. He was in Santa's sleigh! The reindeer were still harnessed to it, and they were feeding on bales of hay. Jack Frost was unwrapping more presents, and the floor was covered with wrapping paper and ribbons.

Rachel, Holly, and Kirsty trembled as the goblins pushed them toward Jack Frost.

"Look what we've brought you!" one of the goblins called triumphantly.

Jack Frost looked up at the girls. "You again!" he snarled, staring at them with cold, hard eyes. "You're always trying to spoil my fun!"

He shook his fist, and Rachel gasped

as she saw the present Jack Frost was holding in his other hand. He hadn't opened it yet. It was still wrapped in its pretty gold paper, and tied with a bow of rainbow colors. It was the third special present that the Fairy King and Queen had asked the girls to find!

Rachel glanced at Kirsty and Holly.
She could see that they'd spotted the
present, too. But how were they going to
stop Jack Frost from opening it?

Kirsty was thinking the same thing as
Rachel. She stared down at
the piles of wrapping
paper on the floor,
and suddenly, an
idea struck her.

"What am I
going to do
with you?" Jack
Frost was muttering,
tapping his long, thin
fingers on top of the
present. "I think I'll put you in my
deepest ice dungeon, and leave you there
for one hundred years!"

"Rachel," Kirsty whispered. "I've got an idea. Can you distract the goblins and Jack Frost for a few moments?"

Rachel looked at her friend curiously, then nodded. "OK," she whispered back.

"Should we take them to the dungeons, master?" asked one of the goblins.

"I haven't decided yet!" Jack Frost snapped. "Now be quiet while I open this present." He lifted the package and shook it. "I can't wait to see what's inside!"

The goblins pressed forward, eager to
see what was inside the package, too. The
goblin who was holding Rachel
loosened his grip slightly,
and Rachel saw her
chance. She
zoomed up into
the air, then
flew straight
for the door.

"Seize her!"
Jack Frost
yelled
furiously.

The goblins
rushed after
Rachel, shouting
instructions and tripping
over one another's feet.

Meanwhile, Kirsty bent down and
grabbed a piece of silver wrapping paper
and a purple ribbon from the floor. While
Jack Frost was watching the goblins,
Kirsty pulled the gold bag with the
magic crown in it out of her pocket and
quickly wrapped it in the silver paper.
Then she tied the ribbon around the
package. Holly gave her a puzzled look.
She had no idea what Kirsty was up to!

Jack Frost was getting more and more angry as his goblins failed to catch Rachel. Eventually, he waved his wand, and instantly Rachel's wings froze in midair. She fell to the ground, landing on top of two goblins.

"Now!" Jack Frost snapped, as two more goblins dragged Rachel to her feet. "I'm going to open this present!"

"Please, Your Majesty," said Kirsty, stepping forward. "Can I say something?"

Jack Frost glared at her. "Make it quick!" he snarled.

"Won't you take pity on us?" asked Kirsty. "We only came here to get this one *very* special present." And she held up the crown, wrapped in silver paper. "It's for the Fairy King, you see, and it's *very* important. Won't you let us take it to him?"

Jack Frost's beady eyes lit up as he stared at the present Kirsty was holding. "A present for King Oberon?" he muttered. "Give it to me!"

"But —" Kirsty began.

"Now!" Jack Frost roared.

A goblin pushed Kirsty forward. Jack

Frost dropped the present he was holding and snatched the other from Kirsty's hands.

Kirsty tried not to smile. She knew greedy Jack Frost wouldn't be able to resist taking the Fairy King's present for himself! Now he was ripping the ribbon and paper away to reveal the golden bag. He put his hand inside and drew out the glittering crown.

"Aha!" he declared triumphantly. "It's a new crown! Well, *I'll* have that!" He lifted the crown and lowered it onto his frosty white hair.

Immediately, Jack Frost vanished!

A Magical Journey

The goblins gasped in surprise and fear. They didn't know what had happened to their master, and they thought they might be next! They ran around the Great Hall in panic. Some tried to hide under the piles of wrapping paper, while others huddled behind giant icicles.

"Great job, Kirsty!" Holly laughed.

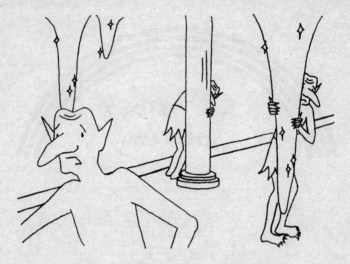

"Jack Frost's been sent straight to the Fairy King and Queen," cried Rachel in delight. She jumped into the magic sleigh and picked up the third present. "And it's time we were leaving, too!"

"But how are we going to get out of the castle with the sleigh and all the reindeer?" asked Kirsty, as she hopped onboard. "They won't fit through the trapdoor where we sneaked in!"

"Don't worry about that," Holly said cheerfully. "The sleigh's magic, you know!" She patted one of the reindeer on the head. "Take us back to Santa, please, my friends!"

The reindeer tossed their antlers joyfully, and began to gallop off down the Great Hall. Goblins jumped out of the way as the sleigh picked up speed. Then it rose into the air, heading for the icy roof.

"Oh!" Rachel gasped. "We're going to crash!"

But, magically, the ice melted away as the sleigh approached, and soon the girls were soaring out of the castle, and up into the clouds. Then the reindeer raced across the sky so fast, that everything was a blur as the wind rushed past the sleigh.

"Here's Santa's workshop!" Holly called at last.

The reindeer had slowed, and the sleigh was floating toward the ground. Rachel and Kirsty peered out eagerly. Below

them, they saw the pretty log cabin that
they had seen in the fairy pool. And there
was a large crowd of elves outside, dancing
in the snow, the bells on their hats tinkling
merrily.

"Hooray!" they cried happily.
"You've found the sleigh and the
reindeer!" As the sleigh
landed, the elves ran
over to pet the
reindeer and feed
them carrots.

Rachel and Kirsty
gasped with delight
as Santa himself
came dashing out of
the cabin. He was in
such a hurry he hadn't
even buttoned up his red coat.

133

"Welcome! Welcome!" Santa called, beaming all over his jolly face. "My beautiful sleigh and my precious reindeer are safe, thanks to you!"

"Are we in time to save Christmas, Santa?" Rachel asked anxiously.

Santa nodded. "Oh, yes," he smiled. "It's going to be a wonderful Christmas!"

"But what about the presents Jack Frost opened?" Kirsty wanted to know. "Does that mean some children won't get anything?"

"Oh, no!" Santa boomed, looking quite shocked. "That would never do! My elves have made plenty of extra presents."

As he spoke, a group of elves ran out of the cabin, carrying armfuls of brightly colored gifts, which they piled up in the magic sleigh.

"Now," said Santa, when the sleigh was full of presents once again. "The king and queen will be wanting to see you. Come with

me and I'll drop you off on my way to
deliver these gifts."

Rachel and Kirsty climbed back into
the sleigh looking thrilled. They were
going to ride with Santa Claus on
Christmas Eve!

Holly joined them, as Santa picked up
the reins. "Let's go, my friends!" Santa

called happily to the reindeer. "We have a lot of work to do today!"

Rachel and Kirsty grinned at each other as the sleigh rose up into the sky again, and set off for Fairyland.

A Fairy Merry Christmas

As Santa's sleigh drew closer to
Fairyland, the girls and Holly could see
sparkling fireworks exploding below
them. Sweet music and the sound of fairy
laughter drifted up to the sleigh.

"There's a big party at the palace,"
Holly said, smiling. "They've heard the
good news."

The reindeer swooped lower, and there
was a shout of welcome from the fairies
below as they spotted the sleigh. Rachel
and Kirsty waved as they saw all their
old friends waiting for them.

"Well done!" called King Oberon as the
sleigh landed.

"You've helped Holly save Christmas!"
Queen Titania added.

The fairies cheered as Rachel,
Kirsty, and Holly stepped
out of the sleigh.

"We brought you
this," Rachel said,
handing the third
special present
to the king.

"Thank you!"
the king
beamed. "Won't
you stay and join
the party, Santa?"

Santa shook his
head. "I'd love to, but I
have a lot of work to do!" He laughed
and shook the reins. "Merry Christmas!"

"Merry Christmas!" everyone called, as the silver sleigh flew out of sight.

"What's happened to Jack Frost?" asked Rachel.

The king looked stern. "He has had his magic powers taken away from him," he explained.

"And he must stay in his ice castle for a whole year before he is allowed to use magic again!" the queen said. "But now it's time to celebrate Christmas, and we have special gifts for all three of you."

She clapped her hands, and two small fairies hurried forward. They carried the two special presents that Holly had brought back to Fairyland earlier.

"These presents are particularly special because they are for the three of *you*!" the queen said.

Rachel, Holly, and Kirsty gasped in surprise, and everyone laughed.

"Since it's Christmas Eve, you can open them right away," smiled the king. And he handed Holly the package that Rachel had just given him.

Eagerly, Holly tore off the gold paper and peeped inside the box. "A new wand!" she cried. "It's beautiful!"

"It is extra sparkly and powerful,"
Queen Titania told her, as Holly twirled
the wand above her head. It left a trail of
magic sparkles behind it, and made the
sweet sound of tinkling Christmas bells.

"It will help you make
Christmas more magical
than ever before."
The queen smiled.
"Thank you!"
Holly beamed.
The queen
handed the other
two presents to
Rachel and
Kirsty. They
couldn't *wait* to
see what was inside!
Rachel managed to open

hers a second before Kirsty, and she
gasped with delight.

"It's a fairy doll!" Rachel said, her eyes
shining. "Look, Kirsty — a fairy for the
top of the Christmas tree!"

The doll sparkled and shone
with magic. She wore a
white dress, which
glittered with silver and
gold, and a sparkling
crown on her long
hair. Kirsty had the
same exact one.

"I can't wait to get
home and put it on our
Christmas tree!" Kirsty
said, smiling happily.

"There's just one more thing," the
queen laughed. "These dolls are magic.

Every year they will bring you a special
Christmas present
from the fairies!"

Rachel and
Kirsty were
thrilled to pieces.
They'd never ex-
pected *this*!

"But we shouldn't keep you any
longer," the king said suddenly. "It's time
for you to go home, or you'll be late for
Christmas!"

Quickly, the girls said their good-byes.
They both had a special hug for Holly,
and then the queen waved her wand.
"Thank you!" she called. "And Merry
Christmas!"

"Merry Christmas!" Rachel
and Kirsty replied, as they
were caught up in a
whirlwind of magic fairy
dust.

"Merry Christmas!"
called all the fairies.

Suddenly, the silvery fairy
voices died away, the magic dust
cleared, and Rachel and Kirsty found
themselves back to their normal size in
the Walkers' yard.

"We did it, Rachel!" Kirsty laughed breathlessly. "We saved Christmas!"

"Let's go inside and put my fairy doll on the Christmas tree." Rachel grinned.

The girls ran inside. Kirsty watched as Rachel placed the fairy doll carefully on the top of the tree.

"She looks beautiful!" Rachel said happily.

Just then the doorbell rang. Rachel ran to see who it was, and found Kirsty's mom and dad standing outside.

"Merry Christmas!" said Mr. and Mrs. Tate with a smile.

"Mom! Dad!" Kirsty cried, rushing over to them.

Mr. and Mrs. Tate stayed for hot chocolate and Christmas cookies, and then it was time for Kirsty to leave. She gave Buttons a cuddle, and Rachel a hug.

"Have a great Christmas!" Kirsty told her friend.

"You, too," Rachel replied. Then she stood on the doorstep with her mom and dad, waving at the Tates as they drove away.

Mr. and Mrs. Walker closed the front door and returned to the cozy living room, but Rachel stayed in the hall for a moment with Buttons. She stared up at the glittering fairy on top of the tree.

Then Rachel blinked hard. Was she seeing things? The fairy had *smiled* at her. And a cloud of magic sparkles had drifted from her wand!

Rachel looked down to see where the sparkles had fallen — and there was a present under the tree that hadn't been there before. It was wrapped in gold paper and tied

with a bow that glittered in all
the colors of the rainbow.

Rachel smiled and pat-
ted Buttons. This really
was going to be the
best Christmas ever,
she thought happily,
and she was sure
that Kirsty felt just
the same.